The Great Big Friend Hunt

First published in the UK in 2004 by
QED Publishing
A division of Quarto Publishing plc
The Fitzpatrick Building
188–194 York Way, London N7 9QP

A Catalogue record for this book is available from the British Library.

ISBN 1 84538 013 4

Written by Hannah Ray
Designed by Alix Wood
Illustrated by Jacqueline East

Series Consultant Anne Faundez
Creative Director Louise Morley
Editorial Manager Jean Coppendale

Printed and bound in China

START
Reading

The Great Big Friend Hunt

Hannah Ray

QED Publishing

Henry was a puppy.
A very small, very scruffy puppy.

He lived on a farm with Cleo the cat. Cleo was sleepy.
She never wanted to play with Henry.
Henry got very bored playing by himself.

When Henry was bored, naughty things seemed to happen. And most of these happened to poor Cleo.

"Oh, Henry," she sighed. "What you need is a friend. That would stop you being bored."

Henry thought this sounded great. There was just one problem – what was a friend?

Henry headed into the yard where the other animals lived.
He stood up, straight and tall – as straight and as tall as
a small, scruffy dog can. In a loud voice he said,
  "I am going on a Friend Hunt.
A Great BIG Friend Hunt.
Will any of you help me?"

Douglas Donkey raised his head.
"Hee-haw! I'll help you, Henry," he said.

"Me, too," snorted Poppy the pig.

"And me!" mooed Clara the cow.

Henry was very happy with
all this help. But there was still one
problem – none of the other animals
knew what a friend was either!

Douglas decided to ask his daddy, who was very wise.

"A friend," said Douglas's daddy, "is someone to talk to."

Douglas Donkey trotted off right away to tell Henry.

"Oh, thank you!" said Henry. "I'm so glad you told me! Now we've found that out, let's keep looking for a friend."
But they couldn't find one, and Henry was starting to feel rather fed up.

Poppy asked her sister Petunia, who was
very clever, if she knew what a friend was.

"Of course I do," replied Petunia.
"A friend cheers you up when you are sad."

"There you are!" exclaimed Poppy. "Now we know even more about friends. I'm sure we'll find one soon. Cheer up, Henry."

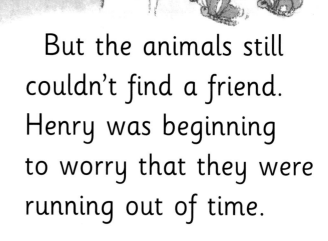

Henry felt much better.

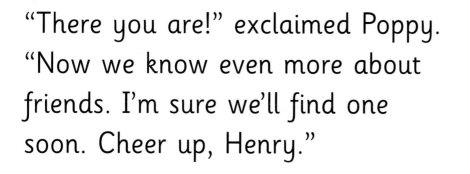

But the animals still couldn't find a friend. Henry was beginning to worry that they were running out of time.

Clara's cousin, Camilla, had come to stay. She knew ever such a lot about ever so many things. When Clara asked her what a friend was she answered, "A friend is always happy to help."

With this in mind, the animals hunted
high and low – but it was no use. They
still couldn't find a friend ...
and it was starting to get dark.

"Don't worry, Henry,"
said Clara. "We'll help
you look again
tomorrow. And the
day after that!"

17

"Oh, Cleo," sniffed Henry when they returned home. "We've hunted all day. We know a friend is someone to talk to. We know a friend cheers you up when you are sad. And we know a friend is always happy to help. But we just couldn't find one."

Cleo rolled her eyes, but she couldn't
help smiling as she said, "A friend
is someone to talk to? A friend cheers
you up when you are sad? A friend
is always happy to help?
You silly, small, scruffy dog!
You haven't just found one friend ...

you've found lots!"

What do you think?

Why did Cleo
think Henry
needed to find
a friend?

Can you remember
the name of
Poppy's sister?

Who else did the animals ask to find out what a friend was?

Why did the animals have to go home?

23

Carers' and teachers' notes

- Look at the cover of the book. What can your child see? What does he/she think the story might be about? Can he/she identify the title?
- Read the story, talking about each picture.
- Look through the book again. Can your child remember each character's name? Point out the names in the text. Can your child identify the letters that start each animal's name?
- Can your child find the mice on each page? Ask your child to make up names for the mice.
- Ask your child who is the biggest animal in the story? Who is the smallest animal? What colour are the animals?
- What noises do each of the animals make? Find the words 'Hee-haw', 'mooed' and 'snorted' in the text. Point out the words in the text and re-read them to your child. Can your child make the noises? What noises would Henry and Cleo make?
- Who is your child's favourite character? Why?

- Re-read the sections of speech in the story, using appropriate voices and expression. Encourage your child to help you decide how each animal would sound.
- The story says that Henry is a puppy. Does your child know the name for a baby pig? (Piglet) What is the correct name for a baby cow? (Calf) If Cleo had a baby, what would the name for it be? (Kitten)
- Check your child's understanding of the text by asking him/her to retell the story to you.
- Look at the word 'friend'. Together, work through the story and count the number of times the word appears.
- Talk about your child's own friends? What are their names? How did they meet? What games does your child like to play with his/her friends?
- Play a game which involves a hunt, for example, set a treasure hunt for your child or play hide and seek.